# Back to School
## with MR. MEN LITTLE MISS

*originated by Roger Hargreaves*

Written and illustrated by Adam Hargreaves

**MR. MEN** **LITTLE MISS**
MR. MEN™ LITTLE MISS™
Copyright © 2018 THOIP
(a SANRIO Company).
All rights reserved.
Used Under License.

GROSSET & DUNLAP
An Imprint of Penguin Random House LLC, New York

The publisher does not have any control over and does not assume any responsibility
for author or third-party websites or their content.

Previously published in 2018 by Egmont UK Limited as *Mr. Men Go to School.*
Published in the United States of America in 2019 by Grosset & Dunlap, an imprint of
Penguin Random House LLC, New York. GROSSET & DUNLAP is a trademark of Penguin Random House LLC.
Manufactured in China.

All photographic images: Shutterstock.com

Visit us online at www.penguinrandomhouse.com.

www.mrmen.com

ISBN 9780593093030            10 9 8 7 6 5 4 3 2 1

Little Miss Tiny was very excited.

It was her first day at school.

She was so excited she woke up extra early.

And she got to school so early that it was not even open when she arrived.

The only other person there was Little Miss Late.

But she was not early.

She was late.

A whole semester late!

When everyone else arrived, they had to hang their bags on their hooks.

Mr. Muddle's bag was so heavy that it bent his hook.

And why was it so heavy?

Mr. Muddle had brought a pack full of rocks to school.

A rock-pack instead of a backpack!

What a muddly old muddle he is.

Little Miss Tiny was looking forward to learning lots of new things at school.

Her teacher was Little Miss Sunshine.

Little Miss Tiny gave her an apple.

But before Little Miss Sunshine could say "thank you," Mr. Greedy had gobbled it up.

In one bite!

**CRUNCH!**

Little Miss Tiny had learned her first lesson of the day.
Don't leave food within Mr. Greedy's reach!

The first real lesson of the day was writing.

Little Miss Tiny very carefully copied the letters Little Miss Sunshine had written on the board.

Unlike Mr. Messy!

And then it was story time.

Read by Little Miss Chatterbox.

Who knew how to make a short story long.

Very,
very,
very long!

Little Miss Tiny was glad to escape out into the playground at recess.

She had a great time on the slide and in the sandbox and she made a friend.

Mr. Small.

He was almost the same size as Mr. Greedy's snack!

And then it was painting time.

Little Miss Sunshine asked them to paint their favorite thing.

Little Miss Tiny painted a daisy.

Little Miss Dotty painted lots of dots.

Mr. Topsy-Turvy painted his cat.

And Mr. Greedy painted . . .

. . . a hot dog!

Little Miss Tiny was very happy at lunchtime.

She got to sit next to Mr. Small.

They had a tiny portion and a small portion to eat.

Half a hot dog and five peas each.

After lunch it was show-and-tell.

Little Miss Naughty had brought her rubber spider.

Little Miss Bossy, the principal, was not happy.

Not at all happy!

Little Miss Tiny was very happy when they went on to math.

Little Miss Sunshine had written a problem on the board.

"What is two plus two?" she asked.

Little Miss Tiny was about to answer "four," but someone answered before her.

"Two plus two equals five hundred and seventy-three point one and two-halves," cried Mr. Wrong.

Oh dear, when Mr. Wrong gets something wrong, he gets it really, really wrong!

And then it was time for sports.

Mr. Silly was their gym teacher.

Nobody could work out what sport they were supposed to be playing!

But it was great fun.

Little Miss Tiny was pretty sad when the bell rang for the end of school.

And that night as she lay in bed she remembered all the fun things she had done that day.

And the next day she remembered something else.

She remembered to take two apples to school.

One for her teacher . . .

. . . and one for Mr. Greedy!

**CRUNCH!**